ME + YOU

BY **DIVINITY ROXX**

ILLUSTRATIONS BY
NaShantá Fletcher

SCHOLASTIC INC.

FOR MOM, DAD, DYMOND, AND RAY, WHO ALONG WITH MY ENTIRE EXTENDED FAMILY, ALWAYS PUT LOVE FIRST.

-DIVI

Illustrated by NaShantá Fletcher/Andrea Brown Literary for Scholastic Inc.

Photos ©: Back Cover: Jay Denes/Divinity Roxx; 11 bottom left: Noel Hendrickson/Getty Images; 12–13: Robert Kirk/Getty Images; 17: Don Mason/Getty Images; 20 composite: Jetta Productions Inc/Getty Images; 22–23: Peter Cade/Getty Images; 24–25: © Santiago Urquijo/Getty Images; 31: www.sciencephoto.com/Offset.com; 32 inset: Jay Denes/Divinity Roxx. All other photos ©Shutterstock.com.

2   185   23

Scholastic Inc., 557 Broadway, New York, NY 10012

SOME FAMILIES MIGHT BE **BIG**

SOME FAMILIES MIGHT BE SMALL

SOME FAMILY MEMBERS LIVE CLOSE

6

AND OTHERS LIVE FAR

EVERYBODY'S FAMILY IS UNIQUE. FAMILIES LOVE ONE ANOTHER, LIKE YOU AND ME. THEY COULD BE

YOUR SISTERS,

YOUR BROTHERS,

YOUR COUSINS,

OR AUNTS,

MOTHERS,

AND FATHERS,

AND GREAT GRANDMAS,

GRANDADS,

AND PAW-PAWS, AND ME-MAWS,

AND PETS...

CUZ PETS ARE OUR FAMILIES, TOO, DON'T YOU FORGET!

IT'S ALL ABOUT LOVE BETWEEN PEOPLE.

FAMILY CAN LIVE
WITH YOU OR NOT,
BUT WHEN THEY
SEE YOU...

11

IT'S ALL SMILES!
AND ALL LAUGHS!
AND ALL JOY!

NO MATTER IF YOU
ARE A GIRL OR A BOY!

I REALLY LOVE TO PLAY WITH MY COUSINS!

OR SPEND THE DAY WITH GRANDMA!

SHE LIKES TO MAKE MUFFINS.

TAKE A WALK WITH GRANDPA.

MY AUNT IS THE COOLEST.

I LOVE HANGING OUT WITH MY DAD AFTER SCHOOL.

FAMILY IS EVERYWHERE!
LOOK UP IN THE SKY,
SEE A FAMILY OF BIRDS AND
THEY'RE ALL FLYING HIGH.

FAMILIES OF FISH SWIM TOGETHER IN THE OCEAN,

AND A FAMILY OF TURTLES WALK BY, SLOW MOTION.

SEE THE LITTLE DUCK FAMILY

AT THE LAKE?

TO MAKE A FAMILY,
A LITTLE LOVE IS ALL IT TAKES.

FULL OF LOVE
ME PLUS YOU
YOU PLUS ME

YEAH
FULL OF LOVE
WE'RE A HAPPY FAMILY...
FULL OF LOVE

ME PLUS YOU
YOU PLUS ME

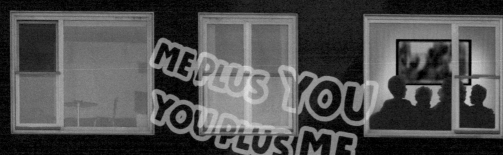

YEAH
FULL OF LOVE
WE'RE A HAPPY FAMILY.

31

I'M SO EXCITED YOU GOT YOUR HANDS ON THIS BOOK! FAMILIES ARE ALL UNIQUE. WHILE MY FAMILY MAY NOT LOOK LIKE YOURS, WE ALL THRIVE WHEN WE SHARE LOVE WITH ONE ANOTHER. I HOPE YOU FEEL THE LOVE I PUT INTO THE SONG "ME + YOU" AND THAT YOU SEE GLIMPSES OF YOUR OWN FAMILY IN THESE PAGES. — DIVINITY ROXX

DIVINITY ROXX

IS A WORLD-RENOWNED ARTIST AND MUSICIAN FROM ATLANTA, GEORGIA. SHE CURRENTLY LIVES IN NEW JERSEY WITH HER FAMILY. WHEN SHE'S NOT TOURING OR WRITING MUSIC, SHE ENJOYS STAYING ACTIVE BY BIKING, HIKING, DANCING WILDLY & EXPLORING THE OUTDOORS.

READ, SING, DANCE... HAVE FUN!

This book makes makes it easy to see: ME + YOU = FAMILY! But that's not all! Here are some ideas for more fun:

♪ This book is all about celebrating people we love. Share the love by reading this book and song with your family!

♪ You will find two kinds of art in this book: photos and illustrations. Can you find examples of them on each page?

♪ This book is also a SONG! Have an adult help you follow the steps below to READ, SING, and DANCE to the MUSIC!

From your smartphone, tablet, or computer:

1. Open your QR code reader (e.g., Android's Google Lens, or Apple's Camera), or download a QR code reader app from the app store and open it.

2. Point your camera at the QR code. You may need to tap the camera button.

3. Wait for the link to open, or tap the pop-up you see.

4. ENJOY!

Scan the QR code with a smart device to access::
https://bit.ly/3okA5po